Pirate School

Level 4D

Written by Melanie Hamm
Illustrated by Stefano Tamberlini
Reading Consultant: Betty Franchi

About Phonics

Spoken English uses more than 40 speech sounds.
Each sound is called a *phoneme*. Some phonemes relate
to a single letter (d-o-g) and others to combinations
of letters (sh-ar-p). When a phoneme is written down,
it is called a *grapheme*. Teaching these sounds, matching
them to their written form, and sounding out words for
reading is the basis of phonics.

Early phonics instruction gives children the tools to sound
out, blend, and say the words without having to rely on
memory or guesswork. This instruction gives children the
confidence and ability to read unfamiliar words, helping
them progress toward independent reading.

About the Consultant

Betty Franchi is an American educator with a Bachelor's
Degree in Elementary and Middle Education as well
as a Master's Degree in Special Education. Betty holds
a National Boards for Professional Teaching Standards
certification. Throughout her 24 years as a teacher,
she has studied and developed an expertise in Phonetic
Awareness and has implemented phonetic strategies,
teaching many young children to read, including
students with special needs.

Reading tips

This book focuses on the *ē* sound, as in h**e** and be**e**.

Tricky and/or new words in this book

Any words in bold may have unusual spellings or are new and have not yet been introduced.

> **Tricky and/or new words in this book**
>
> **recently   devious   raged agent   genius   walks**

Extra ways to have fun with this book

After the readers have finished the story, ask them questions about what they have just read.

What do pirates eat?
When do pirates relax?

This is *Be Bad Pirate School.* You can be bad or go home!

A Pronunciation Guide

This grid contains the sounds used in the stories in levels 4, 5, and 6 and a guide on how to say them.

/ă/ as in pat	/ā/ as in pay	/âr/ as in care	/ä/ as in father
/b/ as in bib	/ch/ as in church	/d/ as in deed/ milled	/ĕ/ as in pet
/ē/ as in bee	/f/ as in fife/ phase/ rough	/g/ as in gag	/h/ as in hat
/hw/ as in which	/ĭ/ as in pit	/ī/ as in pie/ by	/îr/ as in pier
/j/ as in judge	/k/ as in kick/ cat/ pique	/l/ as in lid/ needle (nēd'l)	/m/ as in mom
/n/ as in no/ sudden (sŭd'n)	/ng/ as in thing	/ŏ/ as in pot	/ō/ as in toe
/ô/ as in caught/ paw/ for/ horrid/ hoarse	/oi/ as in noise	/o͝o/ as in took	/ū/ as in cute

/ou/ as in out	/p/ as in pop	/r/ as in roar	/s/ as in sauce
/sh/ as in ship/ dish	/t/ as in tight/ stopped	/th/ as in thin	/th/ as in this
/ŭ/ as in cut	/ûr/ as in urge/ term/ firm/ word/ heard	/v/ as in valve	/w/ as in with
/y/ as in yes	/z/ as in zebra/ xylem	/zh/ as in vision/ pleasure/ garage	/ə/ as in about/ item/ edible/ gallop/ circus
/ər/ as in butter			

Be careful not to add an /uh/ sound to /s/, /t/, /p/, /c/, /h/, /r/, /m/, /d/, /g/, /l/, /f/ and /b/. For example, say /fff/ not /fuh/ and /sss/ not /suh/.

Behold, Captain Ego.

He was feared on all the seven seas.
No pirate was his equal.

Recently Captain Ego
retired from being a full-time
pirate and established the
Be Bad Pirate School.

He began his first lesson
with this refrain,
"If ye wants to be a pirate,
Be a demon of the sea.
Devious, revolting,
that's how we pirates be!"

"Tell me how pirates behave,"
Captain Ego demanded.
"Pirates send e-mails," said Peter.
"No!" hollered Captain Ego.
"Pirates detest e-mails."

"Pirates keep lemurs," said Leon.
"No!" shouted Captain Ego.
"Pirates keep parrots."

"Pirates relax in the
evening," said Eli.
"No!" screamed Captain Ego.
"Pirates never relax."

"Pirates are frequently
vegan," said Felix.
"No!" bellowed Captain Ego.
"Pirates eat everything."

"Pirates dress in
sequins," said Evie.
"No!" **raged** Captain Ego.
"Pirates find sequins repulsive.

Repeat after me,
"If ye wants to be a pirate,
Be a demon of the sea.
Devious, revolting,
that's how we pirates be!"

"I don't want to be a pirate," said Leon. "I want to be a secret **agent**."

"I want to be a superhero," said Peter.

"I want to be a genius," said Eli.
"An evil **genius**?" said bewildered
Captain Ego.

"No, I want to study meteors," said Eli.

Captain Ego felt betrayed.

"This is *Be Bad Pirate School*.
You rethinks or
you **walks** the plank!"
"No, we will not!" said the class.

"You walks the plank," they said.
So it was fun to behave like
pirates after all!

OVER 48 TITLES IN SIX LEVELS
Betty Franchi recommends...

Other titles to enjoy from Level 4

The Maze — 978 1 84898 771 5

Fairy Fay's Bad Day — 978 1 84898 772 2

Eve the Knight — 978 1 84898 773 9

Some titles from Level 5

Snapped by Sam! — 978 1 84898 775 3

Max's Trip — 978 1 84898 776 0

George the Genius Gerbil — 978 1 84898 777 7

Some titles from Level 6

What Wally Wanted — 978 1 84898 779 1

Superhero Ed! — 978 1 84898 780 7

The Robot Bop — 978 1 84898 782 1

An Hachette Company
First Published in the United States by TickTock, an imprint of Octopus Publishing Group.
www.octopusbooksusa.com

Copyright © Octopus Publishing Group Ltd 2013

Distributed in the US by
Hachette Book Group USA
237 Park Avenue, New York NY 10017, USA

Distributed in Canada by
Canadian Manda Group
165 Dufferin Street, Toronto, Ontario, Canada M6K 3H6

ISBN 978 1 84898 774 6

Printed and bound in China
10 9 8 7 6 5 4 3 2 1